Secret PRINCESSES

With special thanks to Anne Marie Ryan

To Robert Williams – here's to many more amazing holidays!

ORCHARD BOOKS

First published in Great Britain in 2017 by The Watts Publishing Group

1 3 5 7 9 10 8 6 4 2

A CIP catalogue record for this book
is available from the British Library.

ISBN 978 1 40834 378 4

Printed and bound in Great Britain by Clays Ltd, St Ives plc

The paper and board used in this book are made from wood from responsible sources.

Orchard Books
An imprint of
Hachette Children's Group
Part of The Watts Publishing Group Limited
Carmelite House
50 Victoria Embankment
London EC4Y 0DZ

An Hachette UK Company
www.hachette.co.uk
www.hachettechildrens.co.uk

Series created by Hothouse Fiction
www.hothousefiction.com

Royal Holiday

ROSIE BANKS

Wishing Star Palace

The Secret Princess Promise

"I promise that I will be kind and brave,
Using my magic to help and save,
Granting wishes and doing my best,
To make people smile and bring happiness."

Story One

CHAPTER ONE

Summer Fun

"Is there any more chilli, Dad?" Charlotte Williams asked, scooping up the last of her dinner. "It's really yummy!"

"There's something about a campfire that makes everything taste better," her father said with a smile, spooning another helping of the spicy stew into Charlotte's plastic bowl.

"Me too!" said her little brother, Liam.

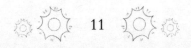

"Me three!" piped up his twin, Harvey.

"I guess everyone worked up an appetite today," Charlotte's mother said, chuckling.

Charlotte and her family were on their summer holiday in Arizona. They had driven all the way there from their home in California. Today they had hiked down to the bottom of the Grand Canyon, where they were camping overnight. The hike had been amazing, but Charlotte's legs were really tired now!

Charlotte gazed around her. The canyon's steep rock walls glowed orange in the sunset, and the sky was a dusky purple, streaked with pink clouds. She'd thought the desert would be dry and dusty, but it was bursting with colour and life.

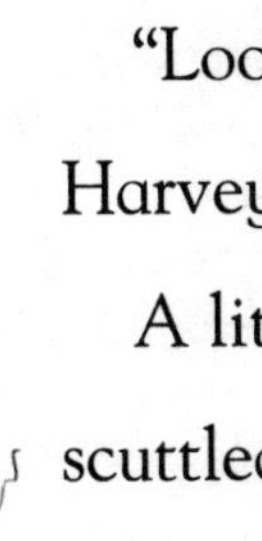

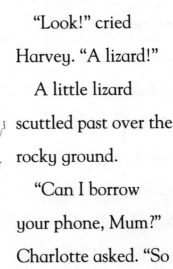

"Look!" cried Harvey. "A lizard!"

A little lizard scuttled past over the rocky ground.

"Can I borrow your phone, Mum?" Charlotte asked. "So I can take a picture to show Mia."

Charlotte quickly snapped a photo of the lizard as it basked on a rock. Then she took a selfie with the canyon in the background, her brown curls shining in the setting sun's rays.

"You can email those to Mia when we get home," Charlotte's mum said. "I'm sure you'll have lots to tell her."

Mia Thompson was Charlotte's best friend, who lived in England. She loved all animals – even scaly reptiles – and knew lots about them. Not long ago, Charlotte's family had moved to

California. She'd been really sad to leave her best friend, but they still spoke all the time.

When everyone had finished their chilli, Liam yawned and Harvey rubbed his eyes.

Dad stood up and put out the campfire. "I think we all need an early night," he said.

They carried their plates and cutlery into the cosy log cabin where they were spending the night. After washing the dishes, Charlotte and her brothers got ready for bed.

Soon, Liam and Harvey were snoring softly, but Charlotte couldn't sleep. There were so many things she wanted to tell Mia about – the rafting trip they'd taken, the eagle she'd seen soaring in the sky and how Harvey had accidentally sat on a prickly cactus!

But maybe she wouldn't have to email her, because Charlotte and her best friend shared a wonderful secret … They were both training to become Secret Princesses, who used magic to make people's wishes come true!

Charlotte felt under her pyjama top and pulled out a gold necklace with a pendant shaped like half a heart. Mia had a matching necklace, with the other half of the heart. Charlotte peeked under the bedcovers and her heart pounded with excitement. Her pendant was glowing!

Holding the pendant, Charlotte whispered, "I wish I could see Mia."

The light from the pendant grew brighter and swirled around Charlotte. She felt herself being swept away, but she wasn't worried about her family missing her. Thanks to the magic, no time would pass while she was gone.

A moment later, Charlotte landed in a lush, green garden. Her pyjamas had been transformed into a floaty pink princess dress and a diamond tiara rested on her curls. She was back at Wishing Star Palace!

The beautiful palace rose up from the clouds, pink roses climbing up its white walls and purple flags fluttering from its four towers.

Even though she had come here before, Charlotte couldn't help gasping. The palace looked so beautiful, especially on a lovely, sunny day. But the best sight of all was a girl with long, blonde hair, who was studying a note pinned to the palace's door.

"Mia!" cried Charlotte, running over to hug her best friend.

Mia's blue eyes sparkled as she returned the hug. "Today was the last day of school before the summer holidays and I didn't think it could get any better – but I was wrong!"

"What does the note say?" Charlotte asked.

"It's from Alice," Mia said, and read it out.

"Welcome back, girls! Use your ruby slippers to come and join us at the palace swimming pool."

"I didn't know Wishing Star Palace *had* a pool," said Charlotte, her brown eyes wide.

"Of course it does," said Mia, grinning.

"It's the most perfect place in the world!"

Charlotte glanced down at the glittering ruby slippers on her feet. Mia, who was wearing her pretty gold princess dress, had a matching pair. They had recently earned them for completing the second stage of their Secret Princess training. The slippers appeared whenever the girls arrived at the palace and could take them anywhere they wanted to go in a flash. Charlotte couldn't wait to use them!

"I hope Princess Poison hasn't been causing trouble again," said Mia, twirling her hair anxiously.

Princess Poison had once been a Secret Princess, but she had been banished from Wishing Star Palace because she'd used her magic to grant wishes for herself instead of helping others. Now she tried to spoil wishes – and whenever she did, she got more powerful. She hated the Secret Princesses and was always trying to stop them.

"If she has, we'll just have to stop her," Charlotte said. "So let's hurry up and find out why the princesses asked us to come!"

"OK, here goes," said Mia, reaching for Charlotte's hands.

Eyes shining with excitement, they clicked their sparkling heels together and said: “The swimming pool!”

There was a flash of light and they rose into the air, soaring high above the palace!

CHAPTER TWO
A Pool Party

Their magic shoes set the girls down by the edge of the most amazing swimming pool Charlotte had ever seen. Surrounded by palm trees, it was filled with crystal-clear turquoise water. A jewelled mosaic of leaping dolphins glittered at the bottom of the pool. A waterfall cascaded into the pool and fountains sprayed jets of water in the air.

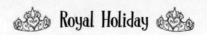

"Oh my gosh!" Mia gasped. "The pool's shaped like a crown!"

There were water flumes and diving boards leading to the main pool. Princess Evie, who had dark hair and wore a green bikini, suddenly came shooting down one of the nearby slides and landed in the water with an enormous splash.

"Hey!" laughed Princess Anna, who was floating on an inflatable throne.

Most of the Secret Princesses were in the pool. Princess Ella, who was a vet, was relaxing on an inflatable shaped like a swan. Princess Sylvie, in a red bikini exactly the same shade as her hair, was paddling with a rubber ring shaped like a doughnut.

"Hi, girls," called Princess Kiko, waving to them from the diving board. She raised her arms, bounced twice, then did a perfect somersault in the air. The water barely rippled when she plunged in.

"Wow!" Charlotte said. Princess Kiko was a gymnast, so it made sense that she was really good at diving too.

Princess Alice, who was sitting on a sun lounger and strumming her guitar, got up to greet them. "You made it!" she said, giving them both a hug.

The girls had known Alice for years. She had been their babysitter before she had won a TV talent show and become a famous pop star. Alice had given them their magic necklaces and shown them that they had the potential to become Secret Princesses.

"Thanks to our new shoes!" Charlotte said, grinning.

Princess Cara, who was sunbathing in a tropical-print swimsuit and funky sunglasses, stood up and stretched. "Ruby slippers are great for travelling, but they aren't exactly pool wear." She smiled at the girls. "Let's see what I can do about your outfits."

As well as being kind, brave and loyal, each Secret Princess had a special talent that was shown on her necklace's pendant. Princess Cara was a fashion designer, which was why her necklace had a thimble-shaped pendant that sparkled in the sunlight.

Princess Cara pointed her wand at each of the girls and with a flash of magic their dresses were transformed into swimming costumes! Charlotte's was sporty tank suit with a strawberry-pattern print, while Mia's had stars and a ruffled skirt.

"Awesome!" said Mia, twirling around to make her skirt flutter.

"Thanks!" said Charlotte. "I love it!"

"Now you look ready for a summer holiday,"

Alice said, beaming at them. "That's why we asked you to come here today – because we're having our annual holiday!"

"Do you need us to water the plants and look after the palace's animals while you're away?" Mia offered helpfully.

Alice laughed. "No, we're not going anywhere. Our holiday is the one time a year that all of the Secret Princesses take a break from their jobs and hang out together at Wishing Star Palace."

"It's always really fun," Princess Cara added.

"We thought our two trainee princesses deserved a holiday, too," Alice said. "Would you like to join us?"

"Yes, please!" Charlotte and Mia jumped up and down in delight.

"Now, why don't you girls have a swim," Cora suggested.

Charlotte and Mia hurried to the nearest slide. As they climbed the steps, Charlotte said, "This is so cool! I was on holiday at the Grand

Canyon when my necklace started glowing, and now I get to have another holiday here!"

"My family hasn't decided where to go for our summer holiday yet," Mia said. "But nowhere could be as cool as Wishing Star Palace!"

The girls sat down at the top of the slide, which twisted round and round like curly pasta. Mia put her arms around Charlotte's waist and they slid down together.

"WHEEEEEEEE!" The girls shrieked in delight as they picked up speed and flew around the bends and turns.

SPLASH! The girls shot off the end of the slide and landed in the water. They swam over to say hello to their princess friends.

Princess Kiko helped Charlotte practise handstands and somersaults under water, while Mia did jumps off the diving board. Then they raced from one side of the pool to the other. Princess Kiko won easily.

"Phew!" said Kiko, slicking back her wet hair. "You two are good swimmers!"

"Hey! I've got an idea!" cried Alice, picking up her wand, which had a musical note at its tip. "Let's make some waves!" She pointed her wand at the pool, and the water churned with big waves, just like at the beach.

"Woo-hoo!" cried Charlotte. Holding hands, she and Mia jumped to ride a wave.

"Yay!" shouted Mia as they rose up on a swell then floated down it on their tummies.

They had fun splashing in the waves until the water was calm once more.

"Do you girls want to have a ride?" Princess Ella asked them, pushing two sparkly purple lilos over to them.

"Thanks!" called Mia, climbing on.

As the best friends lay side by side and floated on the water, Charlotte told Mia all about her trip to the Grand Canyon. "We saw eagles, lizards and mountain goats."

"It sounds amazing," Mia said. "I'd love to go there some day."

Charlotte gazed up at the palm trees overhead. Through the gently swaying leaves, she caught sight of something floating down.

"What's that?" she said, nudging Mia.

"I don't know," Mia said, as it drifted down to the ground. "I think it's a postcard."

Charlotte grabbed it.

"What does it say?" Mia asked, climbing out of the water.

All of the princesses gathered round as Charlotte read the message:

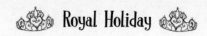

"So the princesses are having a holiday,
But Princess Poison won't get away.
No rest for her, she'll be working like mad.
Spoiling holiday wishes to make people sad!"

"Oh, no!" groaned Ella. "It's from Princess Poison!"

"She's going to ruin wishes so that we can't enjoy our holiday," said Alice angrily.

Just then, all of the princesses' wands started to glow. A wish needed granting!

"She won't ruin our holiday," said Princess Sylvie, picking up her wand. "I'll grant the wish – it won't take long."

"Don't be silly," said Princess Sophie, who was an artist. "You work hard at your bakery and you deserve a break. I'll go."

Charlotte and Mia glanced at each other. "I've got an even better idea," said Charlotte, with a grin. "Mia and I will go. You ALL deserve a holiday."

"We don't have jobs, and we get long school holidays, so it's no trouble at all," Mia said.

"Besides," added Charlotte, "just being together and doing magic is a treat for us."

"Are you sure?" asked Alice. "Princess Poison will do everything she can to ruin our holiday."

"Well, there's two of us and only one of her," said Charlotte. She and Mia were training to be Friendship Princesses. They were the rarest and most powerful type of princess because they always worked in pairs.

"That's so kind of you girls," said Sophie. "But promise us you'll be careful."

"We always look out for each other," said Mia. Alice waved her wand and the girls were wearing their clothes again.

"The Mirror Room," Charlotte said, as they clicked their heels together.

WHOOSH! The girls soared through the air then found themselves in a small room at the top of one of Wishing Star Palace's towers. It was empty, apart from an oval mirror in a tarnished gold stand. The girls touched the mirror, expecting the image of the person they needed to help to appear.

But today there were two people in the mirror! It was a boy and a girl. They looked very similar, with red hair, green eyes and lots of freckles. They were sitting in an overgrown garden, looking bored.

Below their image, a rhyme appeared on the cloudy glass. Mia read it out loud:

"A holiday wish needs granting today.
Help Megan and Rhys, without delay!"

"There are two people to help. I wonder if that means we get six wishes instead of three?" said Charlotte. They had granted a double wish once before, when they had helped two sisters have a very happy Christmas.

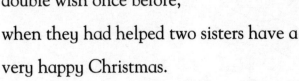

"I guess we'll find out soon," replied Mia. "Are you ready?"

Charlotte nodded and they both touched the mirror. Charlotte felt herself being pulled into swirling tunnel of light, whisking her away from the palace. They were off on another Secret Princess adventure!

CHAPTER THREE

Gran's Garden

The girls landed on a peaceful country lane. Their clothes had changed into sundresses and sandals. The only sound was birds chirping in the hedgerows that lined the road and sheep bleating in the distance.

"I wonder where we are?" Charlotte said.

"This might give us a clue." Mia went over to look at a poster hanging on a nearby tree.

It had an arrow pointing ahead and read: PEMBRY ART SHOW, 3PM TODAY.

"We must be in Pembry," said Mia, gazing around. "But where are Megan and Rhys?"

"Let's go to the village and see what we can find out," suggested Charlotte.

They started walking in the direction the sign was pointing. Across the road, they caught sight of an adorable thatched cottage. When they got closer, they noticed two children in the garden, kicking a ball back and forth unenthusiastically.

"It's them!" whispered Mia, clutching Charlotte's arm.

Charlotte walked up to the house and called out to them. "Hello! My friend and I were out walking and wondered if we could have a drink of water – it's really hot!"

The girl, whose red hair was in two plaits, gave them a friendly smile and said, "Of course!" She hurried off into the cottage, while the boy showed Mia and Charlotte into the back garden. The garden was full of beautiful trees, flowers and plants, but it was badly overgrown.

The boy led them to a table and chairs under the shade of a tree, then the girl came out again holding a jug of water and glasses.

"Thanks so much," Charlotte said, taking a big gulp of water. "I'm Charlotte and this is my friend Mia."

"I'm Megan," said the girl, "And this is my brother, Rhys."

"We're twins," Rhys added.

"Cool!" said Charlotte. "My little brothers are twins. It means you always have someone to play with."

Megan sighed. "That's true, but it would be nice if there were other kids for us to play with, too."

"This is our grandmother's cottage," Rhys explained. "We're staying with her this summer, but she only just moved here. She doesn't have any friends here – and neither do we."

"That sounds pretty lonely," Mia said sympathetically.

"It is," said Megan, nodding. "I really wish we could cheer Gran up and help her make some friends."

Charlotte and Mia exchanged looks. At least they knew one of the wishes they needed to grant!

Rhys nodded. "Yeah, but I don't know how we can cheer her up. It's so lame here! I wish we were having an amazing summer holiday, instead of being in the boring countryside."

Aha! thought Charlotte. Now they knew Rhys's wish, too!

"Maybe we can help you," offered Mia. "What does your grandmother like doing?"

Megan thought for a moment. "At her old house Gran liked gardening."

"She enjoys painting, too," Rhys added. "But she hasn't done any painting since she moved here."

Charlotte stood up and put her hands on her hips as she looked around the garden. If Gran liked gardening, they could start with that! "This is a big garden, but there are four of us," she said. "Should we tidy it up for your gran?"

"Would you really help us?" asked Megan.

"Of course," said Mia. "It will be fun!"

They found some tools in the shed and got to work.

Rhys raked the lawn, while the girls weeded and watered the flowerbeds.

"Gran got these, but she hasn't planted them yet," Rhys said, pointing at trays of purple and pink pansies and bright yellow marigolds.

"Let's do it for her," said Charlotte.

They planted the flowers in pots they had found in the shed and arranged them around the garden.

It was hard work but Mia was right – it was fun!

"What's that?" Charlotte asked, pointing to a little wooden building in the back garden. It looked out over a field of grazing sheep.

"It's a summerhouse," said Megan. "But it's full of junk."

"Why don't we clear it out?" suggested Mia. "It could be an art studio for your gran."

"That's a great idea!" said Rhys.

Together, they quickly cleared out the old junk. Then they brushed off the cobwebs and cleaned the dusty windows. Brilliant sunlight poured into the summerhouse.

"It's perfect for painting!" said Megan, gazing around in satisfaction.

Just then, they heard someone whistle. Coming out of the summerhouse, they saw a short, plump man in walking clothes leaning over the back gate. Mia and Charlotte recognised him at once – it was Hex, mean Princess Poison's servant!

"Here, sheepy sheepies," he called. "Come and get some din-dins!"

He whistled again, and the flock of sheep started trotting into the garden.

BAAAAA! Bleating loudly, the sheep crowded through the gate.

They munched the grass and nibbled flowers. Their hooves trampled the neat flowerbeds and knocked over the pots the children had just planted.

"Hey! Go away!" cried Rhys, trying to shoo the sheep back into their field.

"Stop that!" Megan scolded a lamb eating a rose bush.

Charlotte marched over to Hex, who was chuckling as he watched the sheep.

"You did that on purpose!" she said angrily.

"Of course I did," sneered Hex. "It isn't just the garden we're going to ruin. Princess Poison is going to spoil Megan and Rhys's holiday – and the Secret Princesses' holiday too!" Laughing, he walked off through the field.

The four children chased after the sheep and eventually managed to herd them all back into their field.

Shutting the garden gate behind the last sheep, Charlotte let out a sigh of relief. But when she turned around, Megan and Rhys didn't look very happy at all.

The grass was ruined, with dirt clods and sheep poo littering the lawn. The flowers had been stripped of their petals, and broken pots were scattered about the garden. It looked even worse than it had before!

"I really wanted to make the garden look nice to cheer Gran up," said Megan sadly.

"It will look nice," Mia promised her.

"How?" demanded Rhys. "There's no way we can fix it now."

"Oh yes, there is," said Charlotte. Mia caught her eye and nodded.

It was time to make a wish!

CHAPTER FOUR
Bee-ware!

Mia and Charlotte held their glowing pendants together to form a perfect heart.

"I wish for Gran's garden to look as beautiful as the Wishing Star Palace garden," Mia said.

With a flash of golden light, the garden was transformed. The lawn was lush and green. The flowerbeds bloomed with fragrant violets, sweet peas and poppies. There was an archway covered with pink and white roses, a wooden swing and a little pond with lily pads and a trickling waterfall. Colourful hanging baskets and flowerpots were dotted around the garden. Even the summerhouse looked better – it had a fresh coat of paint and there were checked curtains hanging at the windows.

"What happened?" Rhys gasped.

"H-how did you do that?" stammered Megan.

"With magic," replied Mia.

The twins stared at her in disbelief.

"I know it sounds crazy," said Charlotte. "But it's true. Mia and I are training to become Secret Princesses."

"Princesses?" scoffed Rhys, wrinkling his freckled nose.

"Magic princesses," explained Mia. "Secret Princesses use magic to make people's wishes come true. That's how we were able to fix the garden."

"So, you two are here to grant my wish of cheering up Gran?" Megan said slowly.

Charlotte nodded.

"So why don't you just grant it right now?" Rhys said.

"We're still in training," Charlotte said. "So we can't grant big wishes like that. But our necklaces let us make three smaller wishes to help you."

"And you too," Mia said to Rhys. "We want to help grant your wish of having an amazing summer holiday."

"Is anyone hungry?" called a voice. A smiley old lady with short grey hair and glasses came out of the cottage. She was wearing jeans and holding a plate of home-made biscuits.

"Oh hi, Gran," said Megan, hurrying over to help her. "These are our friends, Charlotte and Mia. They helped us tidy up the garden."

Gran looked around in astonishment. "My word!" she said. "It looks wonderful!" She hugged Megan and Rhys. "Thank you so much, all of you."

As the children munched biscuits, Gran wandered around the garden, exclaiming about how lovely it looked.

"Why doesn't she think it's odd?" whispered Rhys. "I mean – there wasn't a swing or a pond here before …"

"It's all part of the magic," Charlotte said. "Only you and Megan will notice – and you must keep it a secret."

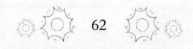

Gran wandered into the summerhouse. "Oh my goodness!" she cried. "You've set up my easel and paints, too!" She came out holding a paintbrush. "The garden looks so beautiful that I think I'm going to paint it. Would you like to do some painting?"

"Yes!" cried Rhys.

"Can Mia and Charlotte do paintings, too?" asked Megan.

"Of course," said Gran.

Thanks to the wish magic, the little summerhouse was well stocked with brushes, paints and canvases wrapped around wooden frames. Gran handed everyone a brush, some paints and a canvas, then she got to work in her new studio.

The children sprawled on the grass with their paints. Mia, who loved art, started brushing paint on to her canvas immediately.

"What are you painting?" asked Charlotte.

"Wait and see," said Mia mysteriously. "But I'll give you a clue – it's somewhere really magical."

Rhys was working on a painting of a flower, and his sister was painting a pony. Charlotte thought for a moment, then decided to paint something from her summer holiday. Dipping her paintbrush in the pink paint, she started painting a desert sunset.

"Gran seems happier already," Megan said.

They could hear Gran humming cheerfully in the summerhouse.

Megan glanced at Mia's painting and gasped. "That's beautiful!"

Charlotte looked over at Mia's canvas. She had painted a gorgeous palace with white walls, heart-shaped windows and flags flying from its four towers.

Charlotte grinned at Mia. They knew that the palace was even more beautiful in real life!

Her smile faded when she caught sight of a tall, thin figure striding over to the garden gate. The person was wearing a white jumpsuit and a wide-brimmed hat with a veil of netting. "That's a weird outfit," Charlotte said.

"I think it's a beekeeper's suit," said Mia.

"It protects them from bee stings. Let's find out what they want."

The girls went over to the gate.

"Hi," said Charlotte. "Can we help you?"

"Why yes, you can," a familiar voice said. "You can get lost so I can ruin the twins' wishes." The beekeeper pushed up the veil and revealed a face with cold green eyes, framed by black hair with an ice-blonde streak.

"Princess Poison!" cried Charlotte.

"I warned those silly princesses that I was going to wreck their holiday," said Princess Poison. She pulled out her wand, pointed it at Megan and Rhys, and began to say a spell:

Buzzy bees,
flap your wings.
Run away or you'll
get STINGS!

There was a flash of green light and a swarm of bees started flying across the field. It was heading straight at them! *BUZZZZZZZZZZ!*

Princess Poison pulled the veil back down over her face and hissed, "If you mess with Princess Poison, you're going to get stung!" Then she waved her wand and vanished.

As the cloud of bees got closer to the cottage, the buzzing grew louder and louder.

"We've got to do something fast," said Charlotte. "Bee stings really hurt!"

"Quick!" said Mia. "Put your pendant next to mine."

The two glowing pendants formed a heart.

"I wish for lots and lots of lavender!" Mia cried quickly.

There was a flash of light and suddenly a big patch of lavender appeared in the field.

"Um, Mia," Charlotte said nervously. "How's that going to help?"

"Watch!" said Mia. Instead of attacking them, the bees changed direction and flew straight to the lavender. They buzzed from flower to flower, gathering pollen.

"Phew!" gasped Megan. "That was close."

"How did you know what to do?" asked Rhys, impressed.

Charlotte put her arm around her friend's shoulder. "Mia knows lots about animals. She's un-BEE-lievable."

Mia rolled her eyes at Charlotte's pun, but Rhys laughed.

"But who was that beekeeper?" asked Megan.

"She's not a beekeeper," said Mia. "Princess Poison wants to spoil your wishes."

"But don't worry," said Charlotte, when she saw the twins' worried faces. "We're not going to let her!"

CHAPTER FIVE

Princess Poison's Trick

"All done!" Gran called from inside the summerhouse.

The children hurried over and found Gran cleaning off her paintbrushes. A watercolour painting was propped on the easel. Gran's skilful brushstrokes had captured every detail of the cottage, and the flowers in the garden seemed to glow with light.

"What do you think?" Gran asked.

"It's amazing!" said Charlotte. The twins were right – Gran was really good at painting.

Charlotte suddenly remembered the poster they'd seen when they first arrived. An idea popped into her head. "Hey!" she said. "There's an art show in the village hall today. You should enter!"

"Oh, I don't know," Gran said, shaking her head modestly.

"You should!" urged Megan.

"Yeah, Gran," Rhys said. "It's really good."

"Well, maybe I will," said Gran, packing up her paints. "But only if you enter your paintings, too."

"Yay!" cheered the twins.

Once Gran had finished tidying up, they all headed down the lane with their paintings. Soon they arrived at the village hall.

A lady in a bright orange smock with a paintbrush holding her long, white hair in a bun greeted them. "Hello. I'm Lydia, the president of the village art club. Would you like to enter your pictures in the show?"

"Yes, please," said Gran.

Lydia helped Gran hang her artwork next to a painting of a rainbow stretching across a meadow.

A man with a white beard and friendly blue eyes came over and peered at Gran's painting.

"I recognise that cottage," he said. "You must be my new neighbour. I'm George Benson – your garden backs on to my field."

"Oh, hello!" said Gran, shaking his hand. "It's very nice to meet you. Those must be your sheep I see grazing from my back garden."

"That's right," the farmer said. He smiled at the children kindly. "Why don't you guys go and hang your paintings up in the junior section?" he said. "My grandkids have entered their paintings, too."

"Gran has made a friend!" said Charlotte as

they hung their paintings. There were lots of good paintings on display, including one of a sheepdog and another of a farmer on a red tractor.

They came to a portrait of a boy and girl about the same age as Rhys and Megan. The children in the picture had brown hair, ruddy cheeks and big smiles on their faces.

"Oh, look," said Mia, reading the painting's label. "It was painted by George Benson. Those must be his grandkids."

"They look nice," said Rhys.

"I still think Gran's painting is the best," said Megan loyally.

Charlotte noticed two people studying Mia's painting – one tall and thin, the other short.

"Maybe those are the judges," she whispered.

But when they got nearer, her heart sank. It wasn't the judges – it was Princess Poison and Hex!

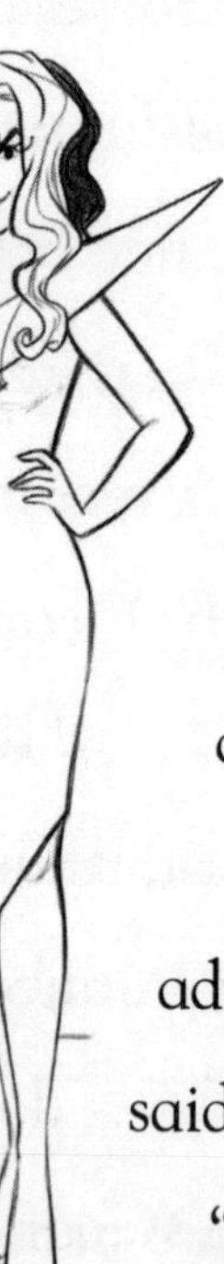

"Not again," moaned Mia.

Charlotte marched over to them. "What are you doing here?" she demanded.

"We're just admiring the artwork," said Hex.

"It's a good thing you have this painting

of Wishing Star Palace, my dears," drawled Princess Poison. "It will help you remember it. Because when I spoil that girl's wish, the Secret Princesses will never let you back there again!"

"That's not going to happen!" said Mia.

Princess Poison smirked and pointed to a man in a tweed jacket who was examining the painting of the tractor. He made some notes on his clipboard, then moved on to the next painting – the one of a sheepdog.

"Let's see what the judge thinks of the old lady's picture now," Princess Poison sneered, aiming her wand at Gran's painting. There was a flash of green light, and the beautiful picture of the cottage was transformed. Now, it was a painting of a rubbish dump!

The vibrant red, pink and purple flowers had become murky browns, mouldy greens and drab greys. The painting showed a rusty car, broken furniture and bin bags overflowing with rubbish. Gran's painting had had delicate brush strokes, but this ugly new painting had thick, messy globs of paint.

"What have you done to Gran's painting?" Megan cried in dismay.

"It looks like a toddler painted it," said Hex, sniggering.

The judge was now studying the rainbow painting, which hung next to Gran's.

"Gran will never win now!" moaned Rhys.

There was no time to lose! Mia and Charlotte put their necklaces together.

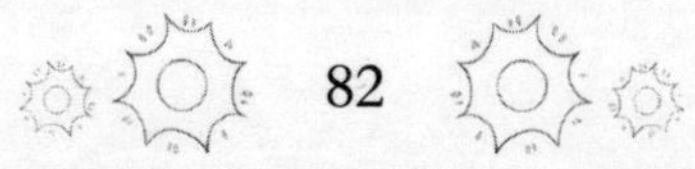

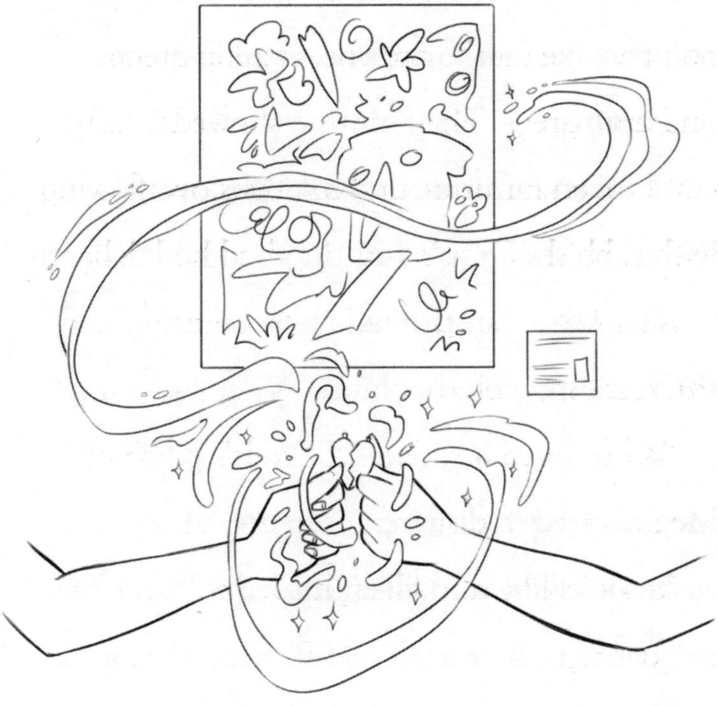

The half-heart pendants were glowing faintly – they only had one wish left.

"I wish for Gran's painting to go back to how it was before," said Charlotte.

There was a flash of light and the horrible painting became Gran's beautiful cottage once more.

"Thank you so much!" said Megan, breathing a sigh of relief.

"Hee hee hee," tittered Hex.

Charlotte glared at him. "What's so funny?"

Hex pointed at the girls' pendants, which were no longer glowing. "You don't have any wishes left!" he said gleefully.

"That's right, girls," said Princess Poison. "You can't stop me now!"

CHAPTER SIX

Picture Perfect

Princess Poison frowned at Gran's painting. "Hmm … I still don't think that painting is quite right. Do you, Hex?"

"No, Princess Poison," said Hex, rubbing his hands together. "I think it needs to be MUCH uglier."

"I quite agree …" cooed Princess Poison. She pretended to think. "Let me see …

Maybe a pile of rotting fish? Or perhaps a stinky toilet?"

Hex giggled nastily and said, "The old lady will be so sad when her painting loses – boo hoo hoo!"

The judge was making notes on his clipboard about the rainbow picture. Charlotte knew he was going to mark Gran's picture next. Just because she and Mia didn't have any wishes left, it didn't mean they could let Princess Poison spoil Megan's wish.

"We've got to do something," she whispered.

"But what?" Mia whispered back.

Narrowing her eyes, Princess Poison pulled out her wand again and pointed it at Gran's painting. She started muttering a spell:

"Turn the cottage into a smelly loo–"

"I've got an idea!" shouted Mia. She raced across the hall and grabbed her painting.

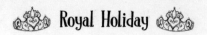

"Catch!" she cried, flinging it like a Frisbee.

Charlotte leapt up and caught it, just as Princess Poison finished her spell.

"Cover it all over with slimy goo!"

Green light shot out of her wand. But before it could hit Gran's painting, Charlotte sprinted into its path, holding up Mia's painting like a shield in front of it.

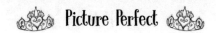

SPLAT! Green goo splattered all over Mia's painting.

"Oh, no," Megan said, staring in dismay at the slime-covered painting. "It's ruined."

"That's OK," said Mia, smiling. "Because your gran's painting is absolutely fine."

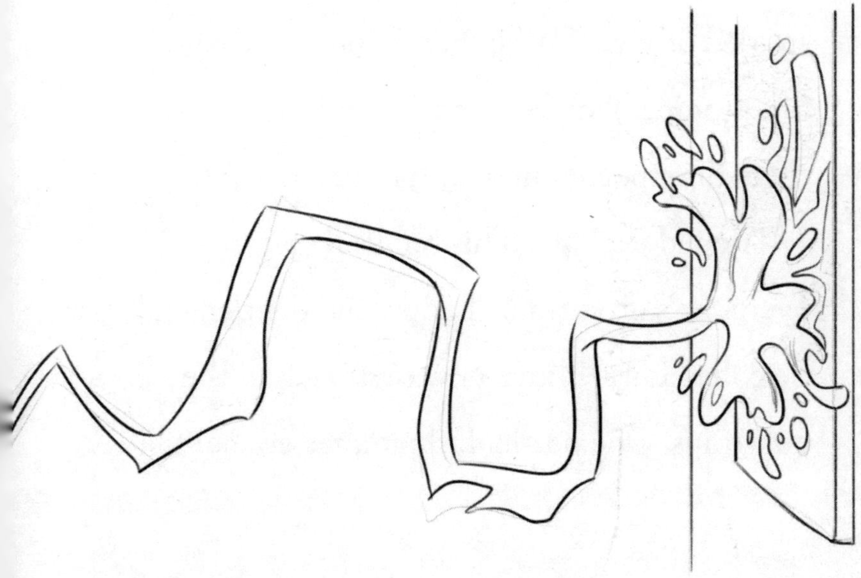

The judge was standing in front of Gran's painting, nodding to himself happily as he jotted something down on his clipboard.

"You idiot!" Princess Poison snarled at Hex. "Why didn't you stop them?" She stamped her foot angrily and the two of them disappeared in a flash of green light.

The judge clapped his hands to get everyone's attention. "Ladies and gentlemen," he called out. "I have now reviewed all the paintings. One particularly impressed me.

The winner of this year's art show is a newcomer to our village – Brenda Evans!"

Rhys and Megan ran over to hug Gran, who looked very surprised. Tears glistened in her eyes and she took off her glasses to dab at them.

"Are you sad, Gran?" asked Rhys.

"Oh, no," said Gran, smiling happily. "Quite the opposite. I've been feeling a bit lonely since I moved to the countryside, but today has changed everything.

My garden looks lovely, I started painting again, and I've made so many new friends. I haven't felt this happy in ages!"

Megan beamed and mouthed "thank you" to Mia and Charlotte.

As everyone clapped, the paintings in the exhibition magically came to life. The sheepdog wagged his tail, the farmer on the tractor waved, Mr Benson's grandchildren cheered, and the rainbow shimmered.

"Look!" Charlotte whispered to Mia.

Mia grinned. They knew that the magic was because they'd granted Megan's wish.

"To present your prize," said the judge, "please welcome local artist Sophie Peters!"

Charlotte and Mia gasped as a lady with

long, dark hair walked into the hall. It was Princess Sophie!

"Congratulations," Sophie said to Gran, handing her an envelope. "I hope you enjoy your prize."

"Oh my!" said Gran, opening the envelope. "Tickets to the Country Fair tomorrow!"

As Megan and Rhys jumped up and down and cheered, Mia and Charlotte went over to Princess Sophie.

"Well done, girls," she said, giving them both a hug. "That was brilliant teamwork."

Gran joined them. "Are these your girls?" she asked. "I'm not surprised – they've got your artistic talent."

Mia and Charlotte looked at each other.

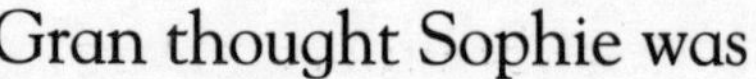

Gran thought Sophie was their mum!

"You must be very proud of them," Gran went on. "They've been so helpful today."

"Oh, I'm very proud of them," said Sophie, winking at the girls.

"Can Mia and Charlotte come to the fair with us tomorrow?" asked Megan.

"Pleeeease?" begged Rhys.

Charlotte held her breath. They really needed to come back because they hadn't granted Rhys's wish yet!

"I don't see why not," said Sophie, smiling.

"Yay!" cheered Megan and Rhys.

"We'll see you tomorrow then," said Gran. The twins waved goodbye as they left the village hall.

"I suppose we should be going, too," said Sophie. She took out her wand and waved it in the air. Before Charlotte could say goodbye to Mia, sparkling light swirled around the girls, sweeping them away.

When she landed, Charlotte blinked in surprise. She'd expected to be back at the cabin with her family. But instead, she was at Wishing Star Palace with Mia by her side!

"Welcome back, girls!" said Alice, who was wearing a fluffy pink bathrobe.

"You did so well to stop Princess Poison," said Princess Ella. She was in a onesie with pawprints all over it.

"We thought you two might like to stay for a sleepover," said Princess Sophie. "What do you say?"

Charlotte was speechless. A sleepover at Wishing Star Palace sounded like the best thing ever! She glanced as Mia, who looked just as delighted as she felt! Both girls started jumping up and down in excitement.

"I'll take that as a yes," said Sophie, laughing.

"We got into our pyjamas early to get comfy," said Princess Cora. "So let's get you sorted out, too." She waved her wand and the girls' sundresses were transformed into pyjamas. Charlotte's were light blue, with buttons shaped like stars. Mia had shorts with lilac polka dots and a matching vest. On their feet were matching fluffy slippers.

"I can't believe we're sleeping over!" Charlotte squealed, squeezing Mia's hand.

"It's been ages since we had a sleepover together!" Mia said happily.

First, they all made their own pizzas for dinner. Princess Sylvie showed the girls how to stretch the dough and toss it in the air.

"Oops!" giggled Charlotte, as she flipped her pizza dough high into the air. It flew up to the ceiling and then landed back down – right on top of Mia's head!

When they'd stopped laughing, Charlotte topped her pizza with mushrooms, while Mia loaded hers with cheese and pepperoni. As soon as they were finished, Sylvie waved her wand and the pizzas were magically cooked!

After dinner, they all played hide and seek. There were so many great hiding places at Wishing Star Palace!

"Boo!" laughed Princess Evie as Charlotte found her hiding behind some long velvet curtains in the ballroom.

Later on, the girls followed the princesses through a door with a gold sign that read 'Movie Room'. It had comfy red plush sofas and an enormous movie screen. They all snuggled up to watch a funny film. Mia and Charlotte sat side by side, their heads touching.

"Who's ready for a snack?" asked Princess Sylvie as the final credits rolled. It was almost midnight, so Sylvie waved her wand and made them a feast! She conjured up lots of bowls full of sweets and popcorn. Then she made everyone a mug of hot chocolate topped with swirls of whipped cream. It was the best midnight feast ever!

When she couldn't eat another bite, Charlotte yawned.

"You two must be exhausted after such a busy day," said Alice, holding out her hand to pull Charlotte to her feet. "I'll show you where you'll be sleeping."

The girls said goodnight to the other princesses and followed Alice upstairs. She opened a door to a beautiful bedroom.

Fairy lights twinkled and pretty pink bunting stretched across the room. There were matching dressing tables with heart-shaped mirrors, a huge double wardrobe, and twin beds with pale pink duvets and canopies of lacy white fabric. It was perfect! Charlotte went straight to one of the beds and climbed under the covers.

"Goodnight, girls," said Alice, blowing them a kiss and shutting the door behind her.

Charlotte turned on to her side, and smiled at Mia, who had curled up in the other bed. "Today was amazing," she said.

Mia grinned back at her. "It was the best! But we still need to grant Rhys's wish tomorrow, so we'd better get some rest."

"You're right. We've got a big day ahead of us." Closing her eyes, Charlotte murmured, "Night night, Mia."

"Sleep tight," Mia said softly.

Charlotte smiled. She knew that she and Mia would have the sweetest sleep ever because this sleepover was already a dream come true!

Story Two

CHAPTER ONE

Breakfast at the Palace

The sound of birds chirping sweetly and the mouth-watering smell of sizzling bacon woke Charlotte up the next morning. Stretching under the duvet, she blinked and saw a white canopy overhead. *Where am I?* she wondered. Turning on to her side, she saw Mia asleep in a matching bed and suddenly remembered – they were at Wishing Star Palace!

Pushing off the duvet, Charlotte jumped out of her bed and bounced on to Mia's. "Wakey wakey, Mia!"

Mia mumbled and tried to pull her duvet over her head, but Charlotte gently shook her best friend's shoulder. "Come on, rise and shine, sleepyhead," she said, with a laugh.

"We've got a wish to grant!"

Mia sat up and yawned. "I thought I was dreaming that we were having a sleepover at the palace. But it was real!"

Charlotte grinned. "Let's get dressed and go find the princesses."

Climbing out of bed, Mia crossed to the enormous wardrobe on the other side of the bedroom. She flung open the doors and gasped.

"Ooooh!" said Charlotte, peering inside. The doors led to a dressing room with rows of clothes and racks of shoes in every colour and style. Best of all, they all seemed to be the perfect size for the girls!

"What do you think?" Charlotte asked, twirling round in a shimmering silver gown.

Mia shook her head. "Too fancy for the country fair." She put on a pair of sparkly gold sandals and handed Charlotte a hanger with a hot-pink layered skirt to try on.

In the end, Mia decided to wear a pretty heart-patterned sundress, while Charlotte chose denim shorts with a red vest top.

"Perfect for a day in the country," said Charlotte, smiling at their reflection in the full-length mirror.

"I'm going to wear my ruby slippers," said Mia, slipping her feet into the glittering magic shoes. "We might need them to get back to Megan and Rhys."

"Good thinking," said Charlotte, putting on her own pair of jewelled slippers.

Following their noses, they headed downstairs and made their way into the kitchen. The Secret Princesses were sitting around a long wooden table laden with crystal bowls of fruit salad, jugs of freshly squeezed orange juice and plates of crispy bacon.

Princess Sylvie was wearing a neat apron and cooking pancakes. They smelled delicious! "Have some breakfast, girls," she said, pointing her wand at one of the pancakes. It flipped up in the air and landed back in the pan.

"Yum!" said Mia. "Those look good!"

Sylvie grinned and handed them each a

plate with a piping hot pancake. The girls sat down at the table. Charlotte poured syrup from a jug on to her pancakes and took a bite. "Mmm!" she said. "Blueberry and banana – my favourite!"

"That's funny," said Mia. "Mine has chocolate chips."

Princess Sylvie winked. "That's because I used my magical recipe – so they're always the perfect flavour!"

"How did you sleep?" Alice asked the girls.

"Really well," said Mia. "I had to pinch myself when I woke up because I thought I was still dreaming!"

The princesses laughed.

"You did really well yesterday," said Princess Sophie. "The twins' grandmother is much happier now."

Alice nodded. "Even when you'd used up all your magic, you didn't let Princess Poison stop you from granting Megan's wish."

"We still need to grant Rhys's," said Mia. "He wants to have an amazing holiday."

"Why wouldn't he?" asked Princess Sylvie, joining the others at the table.

"He thinks the countryside is boring," said Charlotte.

"But it's so interesting!" exclaimed Princess Evie, who loved flowers. "There are so many beautiful plants—"

"And it's home to so many animals," Ella pointed out.

"Maybe we won't even need to use our magic!" said Mia.

"Well, you have three more wishes to use, if you need them," said Alice.

Charlotte glanced down at her half-heart pendant. *We'll need to use wishes if Princess Poison causes trouble again*, she thought.

"Are you going back to the pool today?" Mia asked the princesses, taking a sip of juice.

"No, we're having a pampering day," said Princess Cara.

"Would you girls like to try a princess pedicure or maybe a royal bubble bath?"

Charlotte shook her head. "It sounds really tempting, but we promised Megan and Rhys we'd go to the country fair with them," she said.

"We're worried that Hex and Princess Poison will try to spoil Rhys's wish," said Mia.

"That's very likely," said Alice. "Princess Poison probably remembers how much fun our annual holiday is, and can't stand the thought of us enjoying ourselves."

"We won't let her ruin Rhys's wish – or your holiday," Charlotte promised.

"I know," said Alice, smiling. "She and Hex are no match for our trainee princesses."

Having finished their breakfasts, Mia and Charlotte stood up to leave.

"At least let me do your hair before you go," Cara said. "It'll be quick." She pointed her wand at their hair. In a flash, Charlotte's hair was brushed, her curls even bouncier than normal. Mia's blonde hair was woven into a plait that circled her head like a crown.

"You look gorgeous," said Princess Sophie.

"Thanks!" said Charlotte, grinning.

"Have fun today!" Mia said, waving goodbye to the princesses.

She and Charlotte held hands and clicked the heels of their ruby slippers together. "To Megan and Rhys!" they said in unison. Then the palace kitchen spun out of view as their magic shoes whisked them back to the countryside – to grant another wish!

CHAPTER TWO

Little Lost Lamb

The girls landed with a gentle bump and found themselves in Gran's cottage garden again. It was a beautiful day and the sun was shining. Charlotte gazed happily around at the flowerbeds, the little pond and the archway of roses. She felt a rush of pride at how lovely their wish had made Gran's garden.

"You made it!" cried Megan, running out of the house to greet them.

"Hi, you guys," said Rhys, following after his sister.

"How's your gran?" asked Charlotte.

She could hear singing coming from the summerhouse.

"She's painting," said Rhys. He kicked at the grass grumpily. "And we're bored!"

"Why don't we go for a walk?" Mia suggested.

"A walk?" said Rhys, sounding unconvinced. He looked at Megan and she shrugged.

"It will be fun!" Charlotte said.

"OK," agreed Megan. "I'll just ask Gran."

They ran around to the back garden. In the summerhouse, Gran was painting a view of sheep grazing in the field. "Hello, girls," she said cheerfully.

"Can we go for a walk with Mia and Charlotte?" asked Megan.

"Of course," said Gran. "Just come back by noon so we can go to the fair."

They headed down the lane, in the opposite direction to the village centre. Before long, they came to a patch of brambles. Plump berries hung like purple jewels from the bushes' prickly branches.

"Ooh! Blackberries!" exclaimed Mia.

They picked handfuls of the ripe berries and popped them in their mouths. "Gran says you should never eat berries unless an adult has said it's OK, but she let us pick some of these yesterday," Megan said.

"Mmm! They're so sweet," said Charlotte, standing on her tiptoes to pick some berries hanging just out of reach.

"Yum!" said Rhys, blackberry juice dribbling down his chin.

When everyone had eaten their fill, they continued down the lane.

"Look!" whispered Mia. She pointed to a group of brown rabbits hopping across the field on the other side of the lane.

"Aww! They're adorable," said Megan as they quietly crept forward to watch the wild rabbits grazing on the grass.

"Hey, guys," Charlotte whispered. "What's a rabbit's favourite game?"

"I don't know," said Megan. "What?"

"HOPscotch!" said Charlotte, grinning.

Rhys laughed and said, "And guess what

their favourite type of music is?"

Everyone looked blank.

"Hip HOP!" he said.

Charlotte chuckled and said, "Good one, Rhys!"

"You two are just as bad as each other," said Mia, shaking her head.

Suddenly, all of the rabbits in the field looked up, their long ears twitching. One of the rabbits thumped its hind leg on the ground.

"What's going on?" asked Charlotte.

"It's warning the others of danger," said Mia.

The rabbits streaked across the field, their fluffy white tails bobbing in the grass until they disappeared from sight.

"I wonder what spooked them," said Megan.

"Maybe a hawk – or even just a dog," said Mia. "Rabbits have really good hearing, so they can hear things that we can't."

"I wish we did too," Charlotte murmured to Mia. "Then we'd be able to tell when Princess Poison is sneaking up on us!"

"Actually," said Mia, "I do hear something!"

Baaaaaaaa!

A faint bleating noise was coming from across the field.

They all stood still and listened.

BAAAAAAAAA! BAAAAAAAAA!

"Something's wrong," said Mia. "Let's go investigate."

As they climbed over a stone wall and headed across the field, the bleating sound got louder and louder.

"Over here!" Charlotte cried, sprinting ahead. A little lamb had got its head stuck in a wire fence. Wriggling and twisting, the lamb was desperately trying to get its head out.

"Don't worry, little one," Charlotte said to the lamb. "We'll set you free in no time."

Mia and Megan gently stroked the lamb to calm it down while Charlotte and Rhys worked out what to do.

"I've got an idea," said Rhys. He pulled at the wire to stretch the gap wider. Charlotte jumped up to help him. Together, they made the gap big enough to free the lamb. Then, Charlotte carefully guided the lamb's head out of the fence. At last it was free!

"Good thinking, Rhys," said Megan.

The lamb took a few steps. It looked around the field and bleated anxiously.

"I think it's lost," Mia said. "I can't see its mother anywhere." She picked up the lamb and stroked it.

The sound of slow clapping came from the other side of the fence. Princess Poison and Hex stepped out from behind some trees and walked over to them.

"Bravo, you goody-goodies," said Princess Poison. "I knew you wouldn't be able to resist helping a poor wittle *wambie*."

"Of course we helped," said Mia. "It's all alone."

"Oh, but it isn't alone," said Princess Poison knowingly, and gave a nasty laugh.

Hex cackled and danced about on the spot. "You tricked them, Princess Poison!"

With a sinking feeling, Charlotte slowly turned around and scanned the field. There were no other sheep, but way off in the distance there was another animal. A huge black bull with long, pointed horns was grazing in the shade of a tree.

"Tut tut, children," said Princess Poison. "You should always check for danger before entering a field."

Taking out her wand, she pointed it at the bull and uttered a curse:

There is a bull –
black and large.
Make him
angry so he
will CHARGE!

There was a flash of sickly green light.

Suddenly the bull began to snort and paw the ground angrily.

Princess Poison smirked at Rhys. "You said you didn't want a boring holiday. Is this enough excitement for you?" With another wave of her wand, she and Hex vanished.

The bull lowered his head and charged across the field, straight towards them. His hooves thundered, kicking up clouds of dust.

"Run!" shrieked Charlotte. "Climb over the fence!" But Megan and Rhys were frozen with fear, staring at the bull in terror.

"I can't!" said Mia, who was still holding the lamb. "He'll trample the lamb if I put it down."

"Then we need to make a wish … NOW!" Charlotte cried.

CHAPTER THREE
Egg Hunt

Charlotte dashed over to Mia and pushed their glowing pendants together.

The bull was so close now she could see the ring in his flared nose and the sharp tips of his curved horns. He let out a loud bellow.

"I wish the bull was just a cow!" Charlotte blurted out.

There was another flash of magical light.

The bull was transformed into a black and white cow. It skidded to a stop just feet away from the children.

"MOOOOOO!"

The cow stared at them for a moment, then calmly started munching grass.

"Phew!" sighed Charlotte. "That was close!"

Rhys looked pale. "I thought we were done for!"

"What should we do with this little guy?" asked Mia, picking up the lamb again and stroking its head.

"Mr Benson's farm is over there," said Megan, pointing to a building in the distance.

"Maybe we should take the lamb to him."

"Let's see if he'll follow us," said Mia, putting the lamb down.

"Mia had a little lamb ..." sang Charlotte as they started across the field, the lamb trotting along with them.

They found Mr Benson in the farmyard.

He waved when he saw them.

"There you are, Clover!" said Mr Benson. "I've been so worried about you."

"We found him when we were taking a walk – his head was stuck in the fence," the friends explained.

"It's the strangest thing," said the farmer, scratching his head. "I'd just given Clover a bath to get him ready for the country fair. I turned my back, and the next moment he was gone! I have no idea how my best lamb got out of his pen."

Charlotte and Mia exchanged looks. They knew exactly who was responsible!

"Thanks for bringing him back," said Mr Benson. Then he called out, "Erin! Alan!

Come outside – there's some people I want you to meet!"

A girl and a boy with brown hair and rosy cheeks came out of the farmhouse. The girl was about the same age as Megan and Rhys, and the boy a few years younger. Charlotte recognised them from the portrait in the art show the previous day.

"These are my grandkids," said Mr Benson.

"Hi," said Megan. "I'm Megan and this is Rhys. We're staying with our gran. She's just moved to the thatched cottage over there."

"Cool," said the girl confidently. "I'm Erin. Alan and I live in the village." Alan gave them a shy wave.

"And I'm Charlotte and this is Mia," said

Charlotte. "We're just visiting for the day."

Erin turned to Mr Benson. "Can they help us feed the lambs, Grampy?" she asked.

Mia gasped in delight. Megan and Rhys looked as excited as she felt.

The farmer chuckled. "Of course! After all, they rescued Clover."

They all followed Mr Benson around the barn, to a penned-off bit of pasture.

"This is where I keep all the lambs and their mums," the farmer explained, opening the gate.

"Baaaaaaa!" bleated Clover. He ran over to a sheep with thick, curly wool and a black tail. Clover's mum nuzzled her lamb.

The farmer went over to two lambs snuggled up next to their mother.

"They must be twins, just like me and Megan!" said Rhys.

"These are the two we need to bottle-feed," said Erin, leading the others over.

"Why can't their mum feed them?" asked Charlotte.

"She didn't have enough milk," explained Alan. He took two bottles of milk from a bucket in the pen and handed one to Megan, the other to Mia.

Noticing the bottles, the lambs stood up and trotted over, bleating loudly.

"Just hold the end of the bottle," Erin told them. "They know what to do."

Soon, both lambs were drinking from their bottles greedily.

"This is so cool!" said Rhys as he took over from Megan.

Charlotte grinned at Mia. Rhys was starting to realise that the countryside could be fun!

"Want to try, Charlotte?" Mia asked.

Charlotte nodded and held the bottle. She watched, surprised by the lamb's strength, as it quickly drank every last drop.

"I'm going to give Clover a haircut now," said Mr Benson. "I'm entering him in the lamb competition at the fair and want him to look his best. Now, how would you kids like to go on an egg hunt?"

The chickens lived in a cute wooden house with a ramp leading down to the farmyard. Fluffy hens with orangey-brown feathers were clucking and pecking the ground for worms and seeds. The farmer gave everyone a basket, then took Clover into the barn.

"The chickens sometimes hide their eggs," Alan explained shyly. He was a lot quieter than his sister, but seemed just as nice.

"Hey! Let's see who can find the most," Erin boldly challenged the others.

"Bring it on!" said Rhys, and they all ran off in different directions.

Mia and Charlotte went into the henhouse, where there were rows of nests on two levels.

"Found one!" cried Charlotte, spying a brown egg tucked in one of the nests. A hen sitting on a nearby nest clucked indignantly as she added it to her basket.

She and Mia gathered a few more eggs in the henhouse, then joined the others in the farmyard.

"Got one!" called Megan, discovering an egg in a flowerpot.

"Me too!" cried Rhys, holding up an egg he'd found under a bush.

"Sorry, Maisy," said Alan, as a white chicken with black spots clucked crossly. He picked up an egg hidden in the middle of an old tyre.

"Does anyone have more than six?" asked Megan.

"Nope!" said Erin. "That makes you today's champion."

"Way to go!" said Rhys.

"You can help us gather eggs whenever you like," Alan said. "We hang out at Grampy's farm most days during the summer holidays."

"That sounds great," said Rhys. The boys smiled at each other.

Mr Benson came out of the barn, holding Clover on a lead. The lamb's wool had been trimmed and his clean hooves gleamed.

"We're ready for the fair," he said. "Are you kids going too?"

They all nodded happily.

"I can drive you," said Mr Benson. He handed Megan Clover's lead. "I'll just give your grandmother a ring – we can pick her up on the way." Turning to Erin and Alan, he said, "Go inside and gather up your things."

"Be right back!" Erin called. They went into the house, leaving Mia and Charlotte waiting outside with Megan and Rhys.

"Clover looks so smart," said Mia, patting the lamb.

"I hope he wins a ribbon," said Charlotte.

"Oh, I think that's very unlikely," said a harsh voice.

Startled, the children looked up and saw Princess Poison tottering across the farmyard in a green tweed dress and high-heeled shoes.

"Your fun is going to stop NOW!" she hissed. She pointed her wand at the eggs and said:

"Cover this lamb with messy yolk.
Instead of winning, he'll be a joke!"

There was a flash of green light and suddenly the eggs floated out of the baskets.

"What's she doing?" cried Megan.

The eggs magically hovered over the little lamb – and then cracked! Charlotte, Mia, Megan and Rhys all gasped as the eggs splattered all over Clover. His clean white fleece dripped with runny yellow goo!

"Last one to the country fair's a rotten egg!" Princess Poison jeered.

CHAPTER FOUR

Fun at the Fair

"Oh no," wailed Megan. "Erin and Alan are going to think that *we* made Clover messy."

"They won't want to be friends with us any more," Rhys said.

"That's right," purred Princess Poison. "So you'll spend the summer stuck at your grandmother's, being bored out of your minds!" Cackling, she waved her wand and vanished.

"Hurry up, kids," called Mr Benson from inside the house. "We don't want to be late!"

Mia and Charlotte looked at each other in alarm as Erin and Alan's footsteps echoed from the farmhouse.

"We need to make a wish before they see Clover!" said Mia.

She and Charlotte put their glowing pendants together. "I wish that Clover looked good for the fair!" Mia said.

In a flash of light, the eggs were back in the baskets and Clover was clean again, his fleece even cleaner and fluffier than before. There was a silver bell tied around the lamb's neck with a pale blue ribbon.

"Phew! You guys are the best," said Rhys, looking relieved.

"Doesn't Clover look nice," Mr Benson said, coming out of the house with Erin and Alan. "Let's hope he comes home with a prize!"

The farmer headed over to a red tractor and hitched a big trailer with high sides to the back of it. "Hop on, everyone," he called.

"Wait … we're going to the fair on a tractor?" said Rhys, his eyes wide.

"Is that a problem?" asked Mr Benson.

"No," said Rhys. "It's amazing!"

"Now, who wants to to help me drive?" asked Mr Benson.

"Me!" yelled Rhys.

"Me, too," said Alan. The boys ran over to the tractor and climbed into the cabin.

The girls scrambled into the trailer. There were hay bales along the sides of the trailer for them to sit on.

"Look after Clover for me," said Mr Benson, lifting the lamb into the trailer next to Mia and Megan.

The tractor's engine rumbled to life and Mr Benson drove it out of the farmyard and down the lane to Gran's house.

"I'll get her," said Megan, jumping down from the trailer and running into the cottage.

"Oh my," said Gran, when she saw the tractor. "What an exciting way to travel!"

Mr Benson tipped his cap to her as Megan helped her up into the trailer.

As the tractor trundled along, Erin told the girls all about the fair. "There are loads of fun games to play. And there's tons of yummy things to eat – toffee apples, ice cream, candyfloss …" said Erin.

"But the best thing of all is the pirate ship ride," Alan told Rhys.

"I can't wait to try it!" said Rhys.

Mr Benson drove the tractor into a vast field full of cars. Everyone climbed out of the trailer.

Sounds of music and delicious smells drifted over from the fairground.

"I'm going to take Clover to the livestock area," Mr Benson said. "You kids can go exploring, but listen out for an announcement about when the lambs will be judged."

"Good luck, Clover," Mia said, giving the lamb a final pat.

Gran and the children headed to the entrance. The tickets she had won at the art show got them all in for free and they each got a special wristband to wear.

"These give us free rides," said Gran.

"Cool!" said Rhys.

"Hello, Brenda," said a lady wearing a big sunhat. It was Lydia from the village art club.

"Would you like to come see the craft tent with me?" she asked Gran.

"Oh, I'd love to," said Gran. "Right, you lot, go and have fun!" she called to the children.

They headed across the crowded fairground. There was a band playing rock music, pens full of farm animals, and stalls selling home-made jams and cakes.

"Look!" cried Megan. "Pony rides!"

"Follow me!" shouted Erin, taking charge.

The queue was short and soon they were all on ponies. "You're gorgeous," said Mia, stroking the mane of the chestnut-coloured pony she was riding.

"Mine's called Snowy," said Rhys, who was on a white pony.

"Erin and I have both got ponies of our own," said Alan. "Would you like to come for a ride some time?" he asked Megan and Rhys shyly.

"Oh yes, please!" said Megan.

"You can borrow my pony," Alan told Rhys. "He goes really fast!"

"Cool, thanks!" Rhys replied happily.

Mia and Charlotte grinned at each other. Megan and Rhys were making friends!

When the pony ride was over, they moved on to the games. Megan hooked a plastic duck, Alan did the ring toss and Rhys won on the coconut shy. They came to a stall where you had to knock over a pyramid of tin cans to win a prize.

Charlotte took aim and threw the ball. *CRASH!* She knocked all the tins down on her first try!

"Yay!" cheered Mia.

"Great shot!" said Rhys.

"I play softball back at home," Charlotte said modestly. She chose a fluffy toy sheep as her prize. "It looks just like Clover!" she said, giving the toy a cuddle.

Next, they came to a face painting stand. Megan and Erin got glittery flowers on their cheeks, while Mia and Charlotte had glittery tiaras painted on theirs. Alan and Rhys chose pirate patches and fake tattoos.

"Aaarrr!" said Rhys, chasing after Alan.

"Shiver me timbers!" cried Alan.

Just then, Gran came over with her friend. "Who wants an ice cream?" she asked the children.

Alan and Rhys stopped pretending to be pirates and cried, "Me!"

Gran gave Megan and Rhys enough money to treat everyone to ice lollies.

As they sat on hay bales and licked their lollies, Megan chatted to Erin about horses, while Rhys and Alan talked about their favourite teams.

"They're getting along really well," Charlotte murmured.

"I think Megan and Rhys are going to have a brilliant summer holiday," said Mia happily.

"I hope the princesses are having a fun holiday too," Charlotte said.

"They won't be for much longer," said an icy voice behind them.

The girls spun around. It was Princess Poison!

Charlotte knew they needed to distract the others. "Let's go on a ride!" she said.

"Sounds good," said Erin.

"Look, Alan," cried Rhys. "There's the pirate ship!" He pointed his rocket lolly at a ride shaped like a pirate ship.

"Let's go!" said Alan.

Princess Poison pulled out her wand. "Oh dear," she said, as Megan and Erin ran after the boys. "They're going to be very disappointed."

There was a flash of green light and the ride was surrounded with yellow tape and signs reading "Danger – Keep Out!"

"Nobody is going on a ride today!" said Princess Poison, throwing back her head and cackling nastily.

CHAPTER FIVE

A Happy Holiday

Mia and Charlotte went over to the play area. The others were staring at the broken-down ride, looking very disappointed.

"This is rubbish," muttered Rhys.

"There's still loads of fun things we can do," said Alan. But Rhys looked dejected.

"You said the pirate ship was the best thing about the fair," he grumbled.

"Rhys was having fun," Mia whispered. "It's so annoying that Princess Poison upset him."

"Well, we'll just have to cheer him up again," said Charlotte, taking Mia to one side. She pulled out her pendant, which was glowing very faintly.

"You think we should use our last wish?" asked Mia.

Charlotte nodded, her eyes sparkling. "Rhys wanted to go on a ride, so let's give him LOTS of rides!"

"OK, then," said Mia, holding her half heart next to Charlotte's.

"I wish for lots of funfair rides," said Charlotte.

FLASH!

The run-down pirate ship had been magically transformed. Its chipped sides were freshly painted and the danger signs were gone. Best of all, there were now other rides all around it. There was a helter skelter, dodgems, a carousel and a swing ride.

Rhys gaped at the rides. "Oh. My. Gosh."

He and Megan turned to Mia and Charlotte in surprise. Charlotte winked at them.

Because of the magic, Erin and Alan didn't notice anything strange about the sudden appearance of the rides. They were just keen to try them out!

"C'mon!" cried Alan. "Race you to the top of the helter skelter!"

WHEEEEE!

Charlotte and Mia went whizzing down, one after another.

"That was almost as much fun as the water slide at Wishing Star Palace," said Mia, scrambling to her feet at the bottom of the helter skelter.

When everyone had had a few goes, they tried out the swing chairs.

"Woo hoo!" Charlotte cried, sticking out her legs. Her brown curls flew back in the breeze as her chair spun around in the air.

"Look! No hands!" called Rhys.

"Dodgems next?" asked Erin when the ride came to a halt.

Before anyone could reply, an announcement boomed over the sound system:

"Ladies and gentlemen, we are about to begin the livestock judging. The Loveliest Lamb contest will begin in two minutes."

"We've got to go!" cried Alan.

They raced over to the livestock area and made it just in time – Mr Benson was leading Clover out to the judges.

"I hope he wins," whispered Mia.

A voice hissed back, "One thing's for sure – your princess pals are going to LOSE!"

Mia and Charlotte swivelled around. Princess Poison and Hex were standing behind them. "Once again you have frittered away all your wishes," Princess Poison said, looking pleased with herself. "Now you won't be able to stop me from making that boy's holiday very dull indeed."

"Oh yes, mistress," Hex said. "It will be the worst holiday ever!"

Charlotte looked over at Rhys and Megan, who were chatting happily with their new friends. When the judge handed Mr Benson a blue rosette, they all cheered.

"Go, Clover!" said Rhys, giving Alan a high five.

"Yippee!" cried Megan. She and Erin hugged.

Just then, the twins' grandmother came over, holding a pie and several jars of jam. She smiled at Rhys and Megan. "I like your face paint. Have you been having fun?"

"We've had a brilliant time," said Megan. "We got ice lollies and we went on loads of rides!"

"And guess what, Gran?" said Rhys. "Alan and Erin invited us round to their house tomorrow. They're going to let us ride their ponies." He beamed. "This is the best summer holiday EVER!"

Gran, the twins and their friends went over to congratulate Mr Benson and Clover.

"Look, Charlotte!" cried Mia, pointing to the rides they had wished for. Their signs had magically lit up with colourful flashing lights. Rhys's wish had been granted!

"AAARRRRGGHGHHH!" Princess Poison let out a cry of frustration.

"Sorry, Princess Poison," Charlotte said. "Megan and Rhys are going to have an amazing holiday no matter what, because they have friends to spend it with."

"And so are the Secret Princesses," said Mia.

"Maybe you need a holiday, too," said Charlotte playfully. "You seem kind of worn out."

"Ooooh! Can we, mistress?" said Hex. "I'd love to go on holiday!"

"You don't deserve a holiday, you bumbling fool!"

shrieked Princess Poison, hitting Hex with her wand. Then she waved it in the air and the two of them vanished.

"Oh my gosh!" said Mia, grabbing her friend's arm. The sign at the top of the helter skelter was still flashing – but now it was sending them a message!

WELL DONE MIA AND CHARLOTTE! USE YOUR RUBY SLIPPERS TO COME BACK TO THE PALACE!

The girls grinned, then went over to their friends to say goodbye.

"We've got to go now," Mia said.

"Really?" said Megan. "Can't you stay to go on some more rides?"

Charlotte shook her head. "I'm afraid not.

But I hope you guys have a wonderful summer."

"Thanks so much," Rhys said. "You showed me that the countryside can be fun." He leaned over and whispered, "And that princesses can be cool!"

"We're going to have an amazing holiday – and Gran too," said Megan, hugging the girls. "And it's all because of you two. Thank you so much."

After waving goodbye to everyone, Mia and Charlotte went behind a stack of hay bales. Clicking the heels of their glittering ruby slippers together, the girls said, "To Wishing Star Palace!"

CHAPTER SIX

A Ride to Remember

Charlotte and Mia landed in the garden of Wishing Star Palace, wearing their princess dresses and tiaras. Charlotte sniffed the air and her tummy rumbled. The Secret Princesses were having a barbecue!

"They're back!" cried Princess Sylvie, who was standing by the grill.

"Well done, girls!" said Princess Evie.

She raised her cup of lemonade in a toast. "Here's to two wishes in two days!"

"Did you enjoy your pampering day?" Mia asked the princesses.

"It was lovely," sighed Alice. "I got a manicure." She showed them her fingers. Her nails had been painted bright red, with musical notes drawn on each nail.

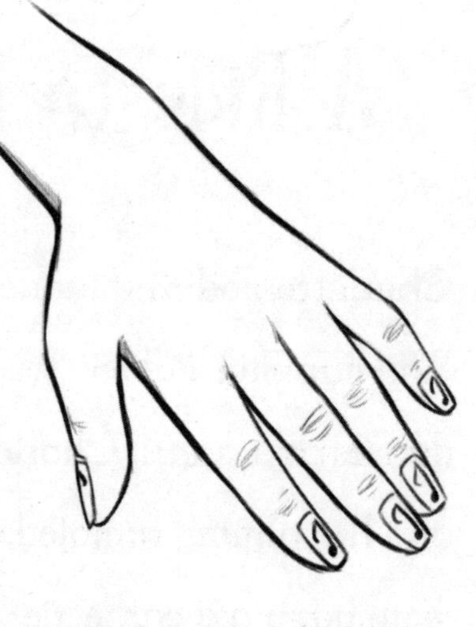

"And I got a pedicure!" said Princess Cara, wriggling her toes. Her toenails were painted midnight blue with glittery yellow stars on them.

"I like your new hairdo, too," said Charlotte. Cara's hair had been coiled into an elegant bun. Curls cascaded around her tiara and tumbled around her face.

"You girls must be hungry after all that wish granting," said Princess Sylvie.

She pointed her wand and two perfectly cooked burgers flew from the grill and landed on buns. "Help yourself."

A picnic table with a red and white checked cloth heaved with coleslaw, potato salad, watermelon and crisps. It all looked delicious!

Charlotte put tomato ketchup on her burger. "I'm so glad we got to come back to Wishing Star Palace to KETCHUP with everyone!" she said.

"Careful," groaned Mia, adding a slice of cheese to her burger. "If your jokes get any worse, they might send you home!"

After eating their fill, everyone played croquet on the lawn.

"Thank you so much for granting the twins' wishes," said Princess Sophie. "It means the world to us that Princess Poison didn't spoil our holiday."

WHACK! Charlotte hit a red ball with her

mallet and it rolled through a hoop. Everyone cheered.

"I'm sorry you girls didn't get to enjoy much of a holiday, though," said Alice.

"We had loads of fun," said Mia. "You should have seen Rhys's face when Charlotte wished for fairground rides."

"Speaking of rides," said Princess Kiko, "have you two ever been on the palace rollercoaster?"

"No," said Charlotte. "I didn't know there was one! But it sounds awesome!"

"It is," said Kiko. "Do you want to have a ride?"

Mia and Charlotte looked at each other, their eyes wide. "Yes!" they cried.

The princesses led them to a part of the garden the girls had never explored. There was what looked like a little train station, with a pink and white rollercoaster waiting at the platform.

"You two sit at the front," said Alice.

"Where are the tracks?" asked Mia, as the princesses climbed into the other cars.

"It's a magic rollercoaster," explained Kiko. "No tracks needed!" She waved her wand and the rollercoaster took off into the air!

The rollercoaster swooped over the palace grounds. They slowly climbed up, up, up to a dizzying height then – WHOOSH! – rocketed down. As air rushed in her face, Charlotte felt like she'd left her tummy at the top of the hill.

It looked like they were going to plunge right into the palace swimming pool!

"Yikes!" squealed Mia. At the last moment the rollercoaster swerved to the left.

Charlotte screamed in delight as the rollercoaster did a loop-the-loop in the air. She threw her hands in the air as they plummeted down hills and twisted around in corkscrews.

When the rollercoaster finally pulled back into the station, Mia was too breathless to speak, but Charlotte turned around and asked eagerly, "Can we go and ride it again?"

"Not today, I'm afraid," said Alice, climbing out of the rollercoaster. "It's time for you and Mia to go home."

"Awwww!" said Charlotte.

"All holidays have to end eventually," said Alice, smiling. "But we wanted to give you girls a souvenir of your stay at Wishing Star Palace." She waved her wand and Charlotte felt something in her hand.

Looking down, she saw that she was holding a model of the palace. It had heart-shaped windows and roses climbing up the walls, just like the real thing. Mia had one too.

"They give you each one wish to use for yourself," explained Alice. "So be sure to wish for something special."

Charlotte thought for a moment. "I wish I could go on another holiday with Mia," she said.

Mia grinned. "That's exactly what I'm going to wish for, too!"

Charlotte hugged Mia. "I had an amazing time," she said.

"Me too," said Mia. "Let's hope our wishes come true soon."

Charlotte clicked the heels of her ruby slippers together and said, "Take me home."

She waved goodbye to the princesses. An instant later she was back in her bed in the log cabin, with her little brothers snoring softly nearby. Charlotte put the little model of Wishing Star Palace on the bedside table – proof of the adventure she and Mia had just shared, though no time had passed here.

Before she shut her eyes, her parents tiptoed into the bedroom.

"Sweetheart!" her mum whispered. "Are you asleep?"

"Not yet," said Charlotte, sitting up in bed.

"I've just had an exciting text message from Mia's mum," Charlotte's mum said, perching on the side of her bed. "They've finally decided where they're going for their summer holiday."

"Where?" asked Charlotte.

"California!" her mother replied, beaming. "They're coming to visit us!"

As Charlotte snuggled back into bed, the windows of the palace model sparkled with light. Her wish had been granted! Charlotte sighed happily. She and Mia had helped

Megan and Rhys have an amazing holiday. They'd shared a royal holiday with the Secret Princesses. And now Mia was coming to visit her in America! Her summer holiday just got better and better. In fact, it was absolutely MAGICAL!

The End

Join Charlotte and Mia in their next Secret Princesses adventure!

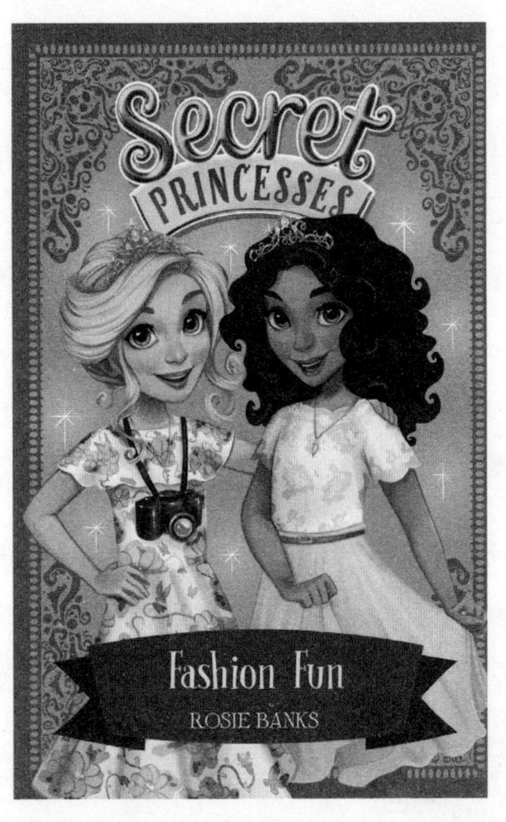

Read on for a sneak peek!

Fashion Fun

"Can anyone tell me the capital of France?" Miss Kelly asked.

Mia Thompson and her classmates were sitting on the carpet having a French lesson. A map of France and a picture of the Eiffel Tower was projected on the whiteboard and the teacher was holding a stripy blue, white and red flag.

Before Mia could put her hand up, a boy with a crop of messy brown hair shouted out, "Paris!"

"*Oui!* That's correct, Thomas," said Miss

Kelly. "But next time please remember to raise your hand before answering," she reminded him gently.

They had only been back at school for a few days but Mia thought that her new teacher seemed kind. Mia's favourite subject at school was art, but she also really liked French lessons – learning how to speak a new language was exciting! So far, Miss Kelly had taught the class how to count to ten and they'd learned a song about the days of the week.

A girl named Emily who was sitting next to Mia waved her hand in the air. When the teacher called on her, she said, "I went to Paris on my summer holidays."

"Would you like to tell us about it?" Miss Kelly asked.

"It was really beautiful," said Emily. "We went to the top of the Eiffel Tower and my mum and dad ate snails!"

"Ewwww!" cried the other children.

Miss Kelly smiled. "France is famous for many things – art, perfume, fashion and delicious food. It sounds like you had a wonderful holiday, Emily."

Mia grinned as she started daydreaming about her own summer holiday. She and her family had visited her best friend Charlotte. Charlotte used to live in the UK and go to the same school as Mia, until her family moved to California. It had been amazing to spend time with Charlotte and to see where she lived now. They'd gone to the beach, visited a theme park, and eaten hot dogs at a baseball game. When it had been time for them to go, everyone had expected Mia and Charlotte to be sad about saying goodbye.

But Mia knew she'd see Charlotte again soon – somewhere even more exciting than California ... a magical place called Wishing Star Palace!

Just before Charlotte had moved to America, the girls' old babysitter, Alice, had given them magic necklaces shaped like half-hearts. Alice had explained that both girls had the potential to become

Secret Princesses – who made wishes come true using magic!

With every wish they granted, the girls were getting closer to becoming fully fledged Secret Princesses. Not long ago, Mia and Charlotte had passed their second stage of training and earned a truly brilliant reward – sparkling ruby slippers that let them travel magically to any place they wanted to go! *I wonder where our ruby slippers will take us next,* thought Mia, twirling her blonde hair around her finger. She imagined all the different places she and Charlotte could visit – a rainforest, a sandy desert, the Arctic circle …

BRRRRIIIINNNG! A bell startled Mia

out of her daydream.

“Break time!” announced Miss Kelly.

Mia’s classmates rushed out of the classroom and charged into the playground.

“Let’s play cops and robbers!” shouted Thomas. “I’m a robber!”

“Want to be on our team, Mia?” asked Emily, waving her over. Mia smiled and ran over to join Emily’s team.

When Charlotte had been in their class, she was always picked first for games. Charlotte was a fast runner and good at sports. Thinking about her best friend, Mia pulled her gold pendant out from under her shirt. To her amazement, it was glowing!

“Er, I forgot my cardigan,” Mia told

Emily. "I'll be right back." She ran back inside her empty classroom and checked that nobody was coming.

When she was sure she was alone, Mia held her half-heart pendant and said, "I wish I could see Charlotte!" The pendant glowed even brighter, filling Mia's cheerful classroom with dazzling light. The light swirled around Mia and then – *WHOOSH!* – whisked her away from school. Mia wasn't worried about missing her next lesson. She knew that no time would pass while she was having a magical adventure.

Mia landed in an entrance hall with marble pillars and a sweeping staircase. Her school uniform had magically transformed into an outfit just right for a palace – a golden princess dress, a diamond tiara and sparkling ruby slippers!

"Looking good, Mia!" a familiar voice called out.

Mia turned around and saw a girl with curly brown hair in a pale pink princess dress. The only thing that shone brighter than her diamond tiara and her ruby slippers was the smile on her face.

"You too, Charlotte!" said Mia, running over to hug her best friend.

"I was at school when my pendant started glowing," said Mia. "We had just gone outside for morning break."

"Cool!" said Charlotte, grinning. "Recess

is the best thing about school." Since moving to California, she had started using some American expressions. Break time was called recess there!

"I wonder if the princesses have gone outside, too?" Mia joked. She peeked into a few rooms leading off the entrance hall, but there were no princesses in the throne room, the dining room or the ballroom.

"I was hoping we could start the next stage of our training today," said Charlotte.

"Me too," said Mia, her blue eyes sparkling. "I want to earn my sapphire ring!"

Like their ruby slippers, the princesses' sapphire rings had magical powers! The blue jewels flashed when danger was near and they glowed in the dark. But the girls needed to grant four people's wishes in order to complete the next stage of their training and get princess rings of their very own.

"I know," said Charlotte, wriggling her fingers in anticipation. "Rings that warn us of danger would be really handy when we're having an adventure!"

Mia's forehead suddenly wrinkled in concern. "You don't suppose the princesses are in danger now, do you?"

To her relief, she heard a familiar voice calling them. "Mia! Charlotte! Come and join us upstairs!"

"Come on," said Charlotte, her hazel eyes

flashing with excitement. “Let’s go and find out why they called us here!”

“Coming!” called Charlotte. She and Mia bounded up the staircase.

They found the Secret Princesses gathered on the landing at the top of the stairs.

“Welcome back, girls,” said a princess. Her strawberry-blonde hair had cool red streaks in it. She hugged them both. “How was your summer?”

“Hi, Alice,” said Mia, hugging her back. “It was amazing.”

“We had so much fun together,” said Charlotte.

“We’re so happy to be back at Wishing Star Palace, though,” said Mia, her eyes shining with excitement. "We can't wait to start the next stage of our training."

"You will soon, I promise," said Princess Alice, tugging a lock of Mia's hair playfully. "We brought you here today because Princess Sophie needs your help."

"Do you need us to grant a wish?" Charlotte asked Sophie eagerly.

"No," said Sophie. She was wearing a paint-splattered apron over her princess dress. "I need help making a decision."

"Sophie's been chosen to show her paintings at a brand new art gallery called the Hexagon," Alice told them proudly, putting her arm around Sophie's shoulder.

"Well done!" said Charlotte.

"That's great," said Mia. The exhibition sounded like a really big deal for Sophie.

"Thanks," said Sophie modestly. "I've chosen some paintings from my studio at home, but I want to include some of the portraits I've painted of the princesses." She fiddled with her necklace. It had a paintbrush pendant, showing that her special talent was art. "But I just can't decide which ones to choose. Will you help me pick?"

Read *Fashion Fun* to find out what happens next!

Mia and Charlotte's Sleepover Guide

Mia and Charlotte love having sleepovers together! Here is their ultimate guide to hosting a perfectly princessy slumber party.

Packing list:

- Cute pyjamas
- Toothbrush
- Hairbrush
- Sleeping bag
- Pillow
- Teddy bear or cuddly toy
- Change of clothes

Games

Here are some fun games to play at your sleepover.

Secrets

How well do you know your friends? Ask your sleepover guests to write down three secrets or facts about themselves on small pieces of paper. Fold each secret and put them in a bowl or hat. Take turns reading out the secrets and trying to guess who wrote them!

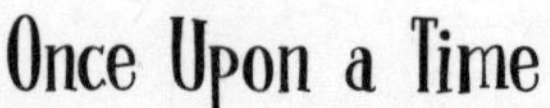

Once Upon a Time

You and your friends can make up a bedtime story together. The first person will start telling a story. The next person will make up the second sentence, saying what happened next. Take turns adding a sentence and enjoy your very own story.

Fun Forfeits

Sleepovers are all about being silly. Challenge your friends to these fun dares – and think up more!

- Imitate a monkey with hiccups
- Say the months of the year backwards
- Hop around the whole room
- Sing a nursery rhyme while standing on one leg

Top Sleepover Tips

- Watch a movie – but it's best to avoid anything too scary!
- Make a den out of blankets and sleep inside it.
- Have a pillow fight.
- Put on some music and dance the night away.
- Don't forget to brush your teeth – especially if you eat lots of sweets.
- If you get homesick, ask your host if you can call your mum or dad.
- Keep the volume down or the grown-ups might get cross.
- Remember to thank your host before you go home.

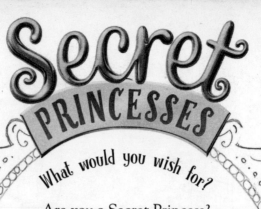